Shoeless Joe
& Black Betsy

Shoeless Joe & Black Betsy

BY

Phil Bildner

ILLUSTRATED BY

C. F. Payne

Aladdin Paperbacks
New York   London   Toronto   Sydney

Shoeless Joe Jackson once played an entire baseball game in his stocking feet. That's why they called him Shoeless Joe.

Some say he was the greatest baseball player ever. Even the mighty Babe Ruth copied his swing.

But what most people don't know is just how Shoeless Joe became such a great hitter. . . .

They say, before Shoeless Joe was to start playing in the minors, he fell into a terrible hitting slump. Worst slump of his life.

No matter what he tried, Shoeless Joe simply could not hit a baseball.

He changed the way he stood at home plate. Didn't work.

Switched from batting lefty to batting righty. Didn't work.

Even tried wearing glasses. Still didn't work.

Shoeless Joe grew more and more concerned. How could he possibly play baseball if he could no longer hit?

Then Shoeless Joe had an idea.

He went to see his friend, Ol' Charlie Ferguson. Ol' Charlie was the finest bat smith in all of South Carolina— and in all the South, for that matter. If it had to do with a baseball bat, Ol' Charlie was your man.

"Charlie," Shoeless Joe said, "I have an awful problem. I can't hit a baseball anymore, and I'm supposed to start playing in the minors. I need your help."

Ol' Charlie raised his bushy right eyebrow. "What do you want me to do about it, Shoeless Joe? I reckon I haven't played baseball in forty years."

"I need you to make me a bat," Shoeless Joe replied, "but not just any bat. I need you to make me the greatest baseball bat there ever was. If you do, I just know I will break out of this awful slump."

Ol' Charlie looked at him. "You're an odd character, Shoeless Joe, but I reckon there ain't no job Ol' Charlie can't handle. You come back in a few days, and I'll have what you need."

A few days later, Shoeless Joe returned to Ol' Charlie's workshop, and Ol' Charlie handed Shoeless Joe the most beautiful baseball bat he had ever seen.

"That's the bat!" Shoeless Joe exclaimed. "She'll definitely be able to hit a baseball. I think I'm going to call her Betsy, after Betsy Ross. Pitchers are going to honor and respect this bat the way they respect the flag Betsy Ross created."

So off Shoeless Joe went. But he still couldn't break out of his slump. A few days later, he was back at Ol' Charlie's workshop with Betsy in hand.

"Charlie, I'm still in this slump. What kind of wood is Betsy?" Shoeless Joe asked.

"Oak," Ol' Charlie replied. "Strongest wood there is."

Shoeless Joe wagged his finger. "I need you to make Betsy out of hickory."

Ol' Charlie raised his bushy right eyebrow. "Hickory?"

Shoeless Joe smiled and nodded. "My last name's Jackson, just like the seventh president of the United States, Andrew Jackson. They called him 'Old Hickory.' Any Jackson who swings a baseball bat must use one that's made of hickory. And Betsy needs to be made of hickory from the north side of a hickory tree. That's the strongest."

Ol' Charlie looked at Joe and said, "You're an odd character, Shoeless Joe, but I reckon there ain't no job that Ol' Charlie can't handle. You come back in a few days, and I'll have what you need."

A few days later, Shoeless Joe returned to Ol' Charlie's workshop, and Ol' Charlie handed Shoeless Joe the most beautiful baseball bat he had ever seen.

"That's the bat!" Shoeless Joe exclaimed. "She'll definitely be able to hit a baseball."

So off Shoeless Joe went. But he still couldn't break out of his slump. A few days later, he was back at Ol' Charlie's workshop with Betsy in hand.

"Charlie, I'm still in this slump. Pitchers aren't even afraid of her. Why?"

"I reckon I don't recall much about pitchers," Ol' Charlie replied. "I only know bats."

Shoeless Joe wagged his finger. "I need for you to make Betsy mean and big and tough."

Ol' Charlie raised his bushy right eyebrow. "Mean and big and tough?"

Shoeless Joe smiled and nodded. "I need pitchers to be frightened of Betsy. I want 'em quaking in their spikes. Rub her down with tobacco juice. Make her dark and scary-looking. And make her big. Real big. Betsy must weigh forty-eight ounces. One ounce for each state in America."

Once again, Ol' Charlie looked at Joe and said, "You're an odd character, Shoeless Joe, but I reckon there ain't no job that Ol' Charlie can't handle. You come back in a few days, and I'll have what you need. But I'm telling you, Joe, sure as the sky is blue and the grass is green, I reckon there ain't much else I can do."

The day before he was to start playing in the minors, Shoeless Joe returned to Ol' Charlie's workshop, and the moment Shoeless Joe stepped through the door, Ol' Charlie raised his bushy right eyebrow and spoke these words: "You're an odd character, Shoeless Joe. I reckon I've told you that each time you've come to see me. My job is done. The rest is up to you."

Then, Ol' Charlie gave Shoeless Joe the biggest and most beautiful *black* baseball bat he had ever seen.

"That's the bat!" Shoeless Joe exclaimed. "That's Black Betsy."

So off Shoeless Joe went to the minor leagues. Playing in Greenville, South Carolina, that first year in the minors, he had a great year. Swinging Black Betsy, Shoeless Joe had 120 hits in only 87 games. At the end of the season, Shoeless Joe got called up to play for Philadelphia in the major leagues.

But things didn't go well for Shoeless Joe. He could manage only three hits in the major leagues. So they sent him back down to the minors.

Shoeless Joe was dejected. So he and Black Betsy went back to see Ol' Charlie.

"Charlie, I don't know what to do." Shoeless Joe hung his head low. "Black Betsy and I hit .346 over in Greenville, but when we got called up to the majors, we couldn't hit a lick."

Ol' Charlie took one look at Black Betsy and raised his bushy right eyebrow. "Shoeless Joe, you're a mighty fine baseball player, and I reckon you've got yourself the finest baseball bat in all the land. But sure as the sky is blue and the grass is green, I reckon you don't know a thing about taking care of Black Betsy. Don't you know Black Betsy needs warmth and love? She needs to sleep in your bed each and every night."

"Thank you, Charlie," Shoeless Joe said. "I'll do that."

Every single night, Black Betsy slept right beside Shoeless Joe. Playing in Savannah that second year in the minors, he had an even greater season. Swinging Black Betsy, Shoeless Joe had 161 hits in only 118 games. At the end of the season, Shoeless Joe got called up to play for Philadelphia again in the big leagues.

But things didn't go well for Shoeless Joe. Once again, he could manage only three hits in the big leagues. So they sent him back down to the minors.

Shoeless Joe was even more dejected. So he and Black Betsy went back to see Ol' Charlie.

"Charlie, I don't know what to do." Shoeless Joe hung his head low. "Black Betsy and I hit .358 down in Savannah, but when we got called up to the big leagues, we couldn't hit a lick. I even did what you told me to do."

Ol' Charlie took one look at Black Betsy and raised his bushy right eyebrow. "Shoeless Joe, you're a mighty fine baseball player, and I reckon you've got yourself the finest baseball bat in all the land. But sure as the sky is blue and the grass is green, I reckon you still don't know a thing about taking care of Black Betsy. Don't you know Black Betsy needs more than just a warm bed? She needs a sweet oil massage every single night. I reckon she takes an awful bruisin' from all them baseballs."

"Thank you, Charlie," Shoeless Joe said. "I'll do that."

Every single night, Shoeless Joe massaged Black Betsy with sweet oil. And every single night, Black Betsy slept right beside Shoeless Joe. Playing in New Orleans that third year in the minors, he had an even greater season. Swinging Black Betsy, Shoeless Joe had 165 hits in only 136 games. At the end of the season, Shoeless Joe got called up to play for Cleveland in the major leagues again.

But before going to Cleveland, Shoeless Joe and Black Betsy went to see Ol' Charlie.

"Ol' Charlie, Black Betsy and I hit .354 down in New Orleans and we've been called back up to the big leagues. I've been treating Black Betsy real good, but I'm worried things won't work out again."

Ol' Charlie took one look at Black Betsy and raised his bushy right eyebrow. "Shoeless Joe, you're a mighty fine baseball player, and I reckon you've got yourself the finest baseball bat in all the land. I can see you're learning how to take care of Black Betsy." Ol' Charlie ran his fingertips over Black Betsy's wood. "When you get up north to Cleveland, you make sure you wrap her in cotton cloth every night. The South is the land of cotton, Shoeless Joe, and a good Southerner must always be true to his roots. Cotton will make Black Betsy feel right at home in Cleveland."

"Thank you, Charlie," Shoeless Joe said. "I'll do that."

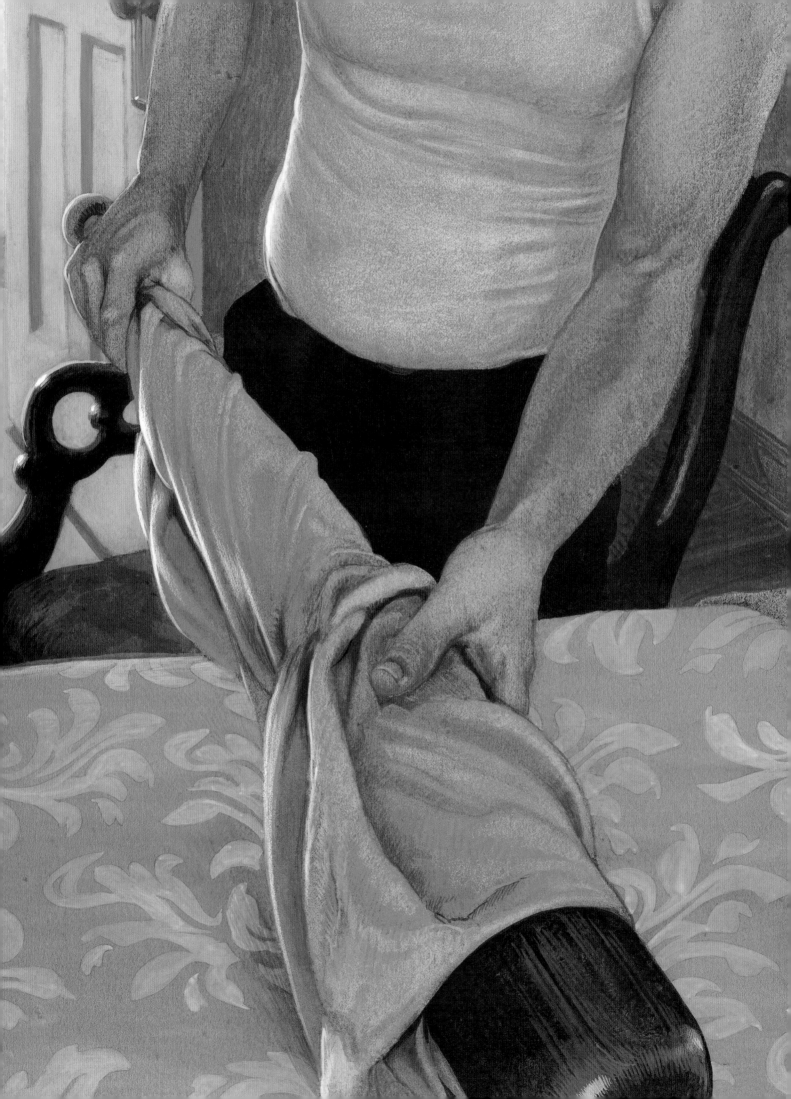

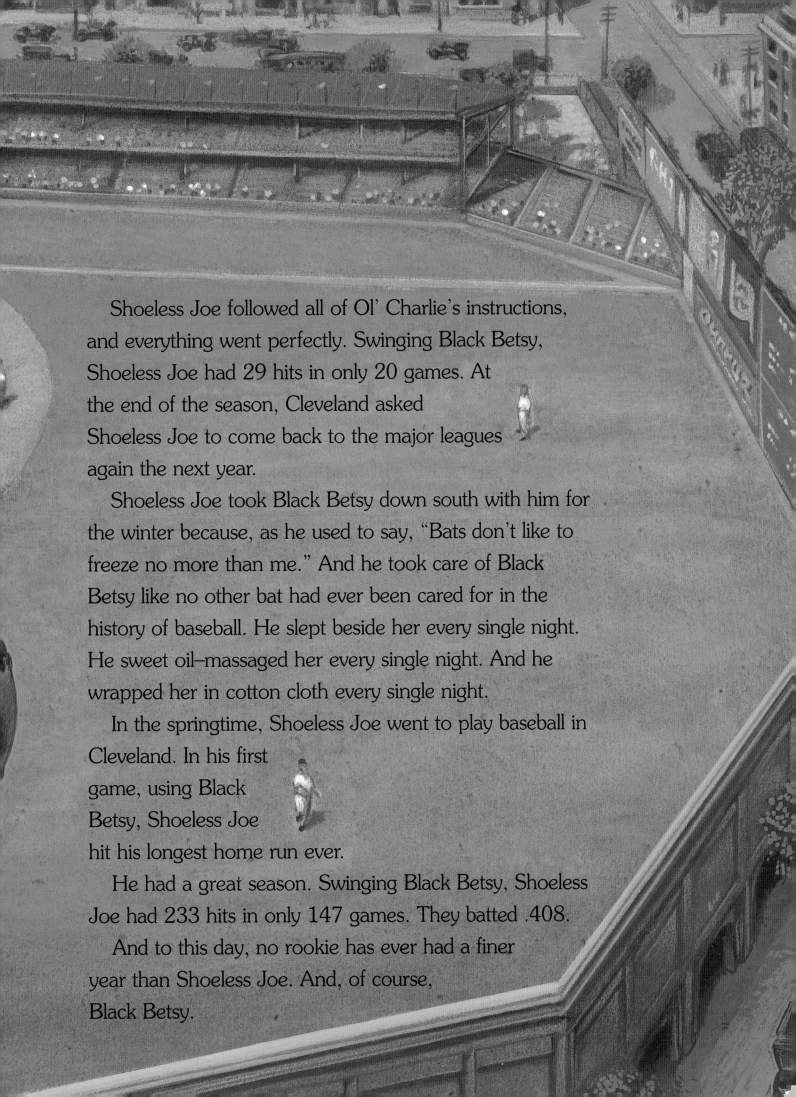

Shoeless Joe followed all of Ol' Charlie's instructions, and everything went perfectly. Swinging Black Betsy, Shoeless Joe had 29 hits in only 20 games. At the end of the season, Cleveland asked Shoeless Joe to come back to the major leagues again the next year.

Shoeless Joe took Black Betsy down south with him for the winter because, as he used to say, "Bats don't like to freeze no more than me." And he took care of Black Betsy like no other bat had ever been cared for in the history of baseball. He slept beside her every single night. He sweet oil–massaged her every single night. And he wrapped her in cotton cloth every single night.

In the springtime, Shoeless Joe went to play baseball in Cleveland. In his first game, using Black Betsy, Shoeless Joe hit his longest home run ever.

He had a great season. Swinging Black Betsy, Shoeless Joe had 233 hits in only 147 games. They batted .408.

And to this day, no rookie has ever had a finer year than Shoeless Joe. And, of course, Black Betsy.

Afterword

Joseph Jefferson Jackson was born in Pickens County, South Carolina, on July 16, 1888. He grew up in the small town of Brandon Mill, just outside of Greenville. Growing up poor and the oldest of six boys and two girls, Joe went to work in a textile mill when he was only six years old. He never learned to read or write.

When he was thirteen, Joe began playing baseball. He was taught by an ex–Confederate soldier from the Civil War, a soldier who himself had learned to play baseball in a Northern prisoner-of-war camp, taught by the Union officers who held him captive.

Joe started out as a pitcher, but he threw the ball so hard, he broke the catcher's arm. So he began playing the outfield.

He earned the nickname "Shoeless Joe" in 1908. While in Greenville, Joe bought himself a new pair of spikes, but the new shoes gave him terrible blisters when he played baseball. When he arrived at the ballpark the next day, he could hardly walk. He wanted to sit the game out, but his team didn't have enough players. So Joe took off his spikes and played part of the game in his stocking feet. During the course of the game, Joe hit a triple, and as he was sliding into third base, a fan in the crowd shouted, "You shoeless son of a gun!" The nickname was born.

Shoeless Joe was also extremely particular about his bats. They were all originally made by a friend of his, Charlie Ferguson, in South Carolina, carved from the wood of the north side of a hickory tree. And because he liked his bats to be black, Joe would rub all of his bats with tobacco juice in order to turn them that color.

Joe took great care of his bats. He would rub them with sweet oil and wrap them in cotton cloths. At season's end, Joe would take all of his bats home with him to South Carolina. He believed bats didn't like the cold winter weather. He also believed each bat held only a certain amount of hits. Whenever he went into a batting slump, Joe would change his bat. Joe's favorite bat was the legendary "Black Betsy," an enormous 36-inch, 48-ounce piece of wood. (While Joe was picky about his bat, and he did insist it be 48 ounces, it was not because of the number of states in the union. In fact, when Joe first began playing minor league ball, there were only 46 states.)

In 1908, Joe signed his first professional baseball contract and went to play minor league ball for the Greenville Spinners, earning $75 a month. He led the league in hitting that year, batting .346. Later that same season, he went on to make his major league debut with the Philadelphia Athletics.

Joe played in the minors again during the 1909 and 1910 seasons. He appeared in the major leagues for a brief period at the end of both seasons. The Athletics traded Shoeless Joe to Cleveland, and in 1911, his first full season in the major leagues, Joe batted .408, the highest batting average ever recorded by a rookie.

In 1915, Cleveland traded Shoeless Joe to the Chicago White Sox, and within three years of the trade, Shoeless Joe Jackson led the White Sox to the World Series title.

Then, in 1919, Joe was involved in the Black Sox scandal, the plot to intentionally lose the World Series. (The previous year, the Chicago players had nicknamed themselves the Black Sox because the team's owner, Charles A. Comiskey, was too cheap to have the players' uniforms laundered.) Joe was allegedly offered $20,000 to help throw the Series, but little evidence exists that he actually participated in the fix. In fact, Joe played an incredible World Series. He batted .375 and had 12 hits, a record for the most hits ever by a player in a single World Series. He hit a home run, drove in six runs, and did not make an error during the entire series.

After the World Series, Joe went to see Charles Comiskey in order to set the record straight, but the White Sox owner reportedly refused even to let Shoeless Joe into his office, not wanting to hear about any players fixing baseball games.

The next year a Cook County, Illinois, grand jury investigated the scandal. Many of the alleged player confessions were mysteriously stolen, and all the players involved were acquitted of criminal wrongdoing. Nevertheless, the new commissioner of baseball, Kenesaw Mountain Landis, an iron-fisted former federal judge, decided to ban the eight White Sox players involved in the scandal.

Joe ended his career with a lifetime batting average of .356. Only Ty Cobb and Rogers Hornsby compiled higher lifetime batting averages. Over the course of 13 seasons, Joe led the league in triples three times and struck out a total of only 158 times.

Banished from the game he loved, Shoeless Joe opened a successful dry-cleaning business in Savannah, Georgia. In the summer, he would play baseball for any team willing to let him. In 1929, Shoeless Joe moved his business to Greenville, near his old hometown. A few years later, when Greenville needed someone to run their minor league baseball team, the city petitioned Judge Landis to allow Joe to be their player-manager. Judge Landis refused to grant the permission.

In 1951, the city of Cleveland elected Shoeless Joe to be a charter member of the Cleveland Sports Hall of Fame. Later that same year, on December 5, Shoeless Joe died of a heart attack.

In the 50 years since his passing, numerous efforts have been made to clear Shoeless Joe's name and have him reinstated into baseball. In 1998, the South Carolina State Legislature passed a resolution asking Baseball Commissioner Bud Selig to lift the lifetime banishment of Shoeless Joe Jackson.

"Shoeless Joe" Jackson

FULL NAME: Joseph Jefferson Jackson

BORN: July 16, 1888, Pickens County, South Carolina

DIED: December 5, 1951, Greenville, South Carolina

BATS: Left

THROWS: Right

HEIGHT: 6'1"

WEIGHT: 200 lb.

MAJOR LEAGUE STATISTICS—REGULAR SEASON

YEAR	TEAM	AVG.	G	AB	R	H	2B	3B	HR	RBI	SB
1908	Philadelphia	.130	5	23	0	3	0	0	0	3	0
1909	Philadelphia	.176	5	17	3	3	0	0	0	3	0
1910	Cleveland	.387	20	75	15	29	2	5	1	11	4
1911	Cleveland	.408	147	571	126	233	45	19	7	83	41
1912	Cleveland	.395	154	572	121	226	44	26	3	90	35
1913	Cleveland	.373	148	528	109	197	39	17	7	71	26
1914	Cleveland	.338	122	453	61	153	22	13	3	53	22
1915	Cleveland	.327	83	303	42	99	16	9	3	45	10
1915	Chicago	.272	45	158	21	43	4	5	2	36	6
1916	Chicago	.341	155	592	91	202	40	21	3	78	24
1917	Chicago	.301	146	538	91	162	20	17	5	75	13
1918	Chicago	.354	17	65	9	23	2	2	1	20	3
1919	Chicago	.351	139	516	79	181	31	14	7	96	9
1920	Chicago	.382	146	570	105	218	42	20	12	121	9
TOTALS		.356	1332	4981	873	1772	307	168	54	785	202

WORLD SERIES

	AVG.	G	AB	R	H	2B	3B	HR	RBI	BB	SB
1917	.304	6	23	4	7	0	0	0	2	1	1
1919	.375	8	32	5	12	3	0	1	6	1	0

For Kevin, a baseball fan ever since Central Park
—P. B.

To the memory of Vada Pinson and all the other great ball players who thrilled wide-eyed kids like me. May there be a day I can visit Cooperstown and find Joe Jackson and Pete Rose where they belong—in the Hall of Fame.
—C. F. P.

Special thanks to Mike Nola at the Shoeless Joe Jackson Virtual Hall of Fame (http://www.blackbetsy.com)

ALADDIN PAPERBACKS
An imprint of Simon & Schuster Children's Publishing Division
1230 Avenue of the Americas, New York, NY 10020
Text copyright © 2002 by Phil Bildner
Illustrations copyright © 2002 by C. F. Payne
All rights reserved, including the right of reproduction in whole or in part in any form.
ALADDIN PAPERBACKS and colophon are registered trademarks of Simon & Schuster, Inc.
Also available in a Simon & Schuster Books for Young Readers hardcover edition.
Designed by Paul Zakris
The text of this book was set in 16-point Souvenir Light.
Manufactured in China
First Aladdin Paperbacks edition March 2006
2 4 6 8 10 9 7 5 3 1
The Library of Congress has cataloged the hardcover edition as follows:
Bildner, Phil.
Shoeless Joe and Black Betsy / by Phil Bildner ; illustrated by C. F. Payne.—1st ed.
p. cm.
Summary: Shoeless Joe Jackson, said by some to be the greatest baseball player ever, goes into a hitting slump just before he is to start his minor league career, so he asks a friend to make him a special bat to help him hit.
ISBN-13: 978-0-689-82913-0 (hc.)
ISBN-10: 0-689-82913-2 (hc.)
1. Jackson, Joe, 1888-1951 Juvenile Fiction. [1. Jackson, Joe, 1888-1951 Fiction. 2. Baseball Fiction.]
I. Payne, C. F., ill. II. Title
PZ7.B4923Sh 2002
[E]—dc21
99-40563
ISBN-13: 978-0-689-87437-6 (pbk.)
ISBN-10: 0-689-87437-5 (pbk.)